Me and My Grandad

Alison Ritchie • Alison Edgson

LITTLE TIGER
LONDON

My grandad is here,
it's my BEST kind of day!
I hop on his back
and we're up and away.

The Kitchen

As we have seen, there were many different people living in a castle. They all had different jobs to do and all had to be fed as well. Castles were often difficult to reach and some were all on their own which meant that a lot of the food had to be produced in and around the castle itself. Animals were kept within the castle walls and there was usually a garden,

too, in which herbs and medicinal plants were grown as well as vegetables. The kitchens were often very big—after all, the cooks had to make meals for so many people. Soups and stews would bubble away over open fires, and meat was roasted on long spits. Most kitchens had tables and shelves, baskets for fruit and vegetables and shovels to keep the fires going. The rubbish and wastewater was poured down a stone chute right into the moat or ditch, or else directly down the side of the hill. The oven used to bake the bread was often not in the kitchen but in a separate bakehouse. Supplies were stored in the cool cellars under the castle. Meat used to be smoked or salted so that it could be kept longer and vegetables were pickled. One of the most important things was the water supply. Gutters and downpipes were used to collect the rainwater and feed it into a storage tank. There would have been a deep well, too, so that there was always a supply of fresh water. If a river flowed past the castle walls, fresh water would be collected by lowering a bucket on a rope. Water was something very valuable in a castle and so things were not washed down that often and only the richest people had baths.

Attack!

Life in the Middle Ages was not always peaceful. But it was not very easy to attack a castle either, even though there were often only as few as twelve men defending it and they would have been outnumbered by the enemy. One of the important things when a castle was 'under siege', as it was called when the enemy was trying to get inside, was that everyone in the castle kept their nerve. After all, it must have been difficult being stuck inside for a long time. Everybody would have been frightened and then there

was the question as to whether the food and drink would last long enough. In addition there was fear of becoming ill as it would then be easier to attack the castle. The enemy even used to catapult dead animals over the castle walls! One of the other great dangers was fire. A fire inside the castle had to be prevented at all costs. All the roofs, the galleries along the castle walls and the gates which were all made of wood, were covered with lime, damp animal skins, cloth or slates so that they would not catch fire if a burning arrow landed on them.

A battering ram was a very big piece of wood on a cart and was used to smash down gateways and walls. Often a metal head in the shape of a male sheep —a ram—was fixed to the front, giving it its name.

Lots of men were needed to attack a castle using ladders. The people in a castle defended themselves with crossbows as well as with ordinary bows and arrows. Stones were the most common form of 'weapon'. Other things were thrown at the enemy, too, such as rubbish and even furniture!

Protected by a moving screen, the attackers would try to dig a tunnel or make a hole in the wall. Wooden towers built for attacking a castle could be anything up to 100 feet high and had a platform at the top for the archers. A bridge-like platform could be let down so that the enemy could climb across into the castle.

To get closer to the walls, the attackers would try to fill in the ditch with wood and stones.

The small openings above a gateway are called machicolations. Usually it was stones that were thrown and only very rarely pitch (tar), oil or boiling water since these things were all too vaiuable to those living in the castle.

18

How to become a Knight

Every knight had at least two horses, one for the battlefield and one for carrying heavy things.

The owner of a castle, who would probably have been a knight himself, needed the help of other knights to defend his castle and his lands. But what made a knight different from other soldiers? There was his horse, and also his armour, sword, shield, and lance. But then there was something else that made a knight so special—the way he set an example and his good manners.

How did anyone become a knight? Training started at a young age. At seven, the sons of knights became pages. They were taught by their father, brother, or a teacher in the art of riding, swimming, archery, and boxing.

No knight could put on his armour without some help. His page was always at hand.

During the Middle Ages, chain mail was an important part of every knight's armour. Its place was later taken by plate armour. A chain mail shirt weighed around 12 kilos and complete battlegear some 25 kilos.

When they were fourteen years old, the boys left home to become valets in the service of other knights who continued the boys' training. They would learn the different ways to fight, how to use weapons, and also how to behave themselves at court. They also learnt how to dance, how to act in the company of ladies, how to eat correctly at table, and how to play board games such as chess. During this time, the young boy would follow his master around everywhere—to the battlefields and to jousting tournaments—he would help the knight put on his armour, and serve him at table. In many countries in Europe, the young men became knights when they were twenty-one. Following a church service the master would present his pupil with a sword. It wasn't until the thirteenth century that knights were appointed by the king who would tap the young men on the shoulder with his sword.

As helmets became bigger and bigger and covered up the whole face, different ways of telling who was hidden under the armour were used. Knights had their coats of arms added to their helmets and painted on their shields.

It was so difficult for a knight to move in his suit of armour that he had to be heaved onto his horse using a special pulley system!

The Tournament

Tournaments were often held at castles and any number of knights were invited. If a castle was particularly big, it had its own special area for tournaments. Otherwise they were held on fields near the castle. The lord of the castle had stands built so that the nobles could get a good view. Ordinary people stood behind the barriers and watched from there. It was very expensive organising a tournament. A messenger would have been sent out to inform all those taking part in good time and the lord of the castle had to provide prizes for the winners which could include a valuable horse, a suit of armour or falcons for hunting.

What happened during a tournament? On the first day of a tournament the knights had to present their helmets to the referee who then decided who could take part. Only knights who had done nothing wrong were allowed to join in the tournament.

The tournament opened with one-to-one fighting or jousting as it is called when one knight rides towards another and tries to push him from his horse using his lance. At important tournaments, jousting could go on for several days.

Each round was announced by a fanfare of trumpets.

The tournament built up to the final event —the biggest competition. Two groups of knights rode against each other like in a real battle. The winner was the group with the most riders still on their horses at the end.

At the close of the tournament, the winner would be presented with his prize by a noble lady. To finish the festival there would be a big party called a banquet and lots of dancing.

The Banquet

Banquets were held in the Great Hall in the keep. Long tables made of planks resting on big blocks of wood were set up and covered in white tablecloths. The table at which the lord sat together with his wife and the most important guests was higher than the others. They had their backs to the wall and could look across the hall at their guests. In those days they didn't have as much crockery and cutlery as we have nowadays. What they did have was not made of china either. Depending on how rich the lord of the castle was, the dishes were made of wood, pewter or even silver. All of the guests had their own plate and spoon. Forks—with just two prongs—and knives were shared but most

things were eaten with their fingers. Although salt was used, it was always placed on the high table where the lord sat. Salt was very expensive and so was kept in valuable containers made of silver or gold, which were sometimes in the shape of a ship. During the banquet music was played and there were performances by dancers and acrobats. Even complete plays were acted out or readings were given from stories written about the knights—which were normally about love and bold and daring deeds. When the feast was over, the tables were taken out and the guests danced the night away.

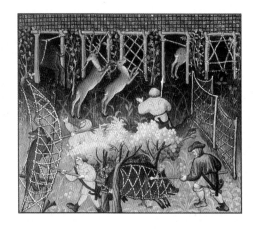

The Hunt

One of a lord's most popular pastimes was hunting. As the animals hunted weren't always eaten afterwards, hunting was more of a sport than a way of finding food. During the course of the Middle Ages, farmers lost their right to hunt—it was then reserved for the nobles only.

The lord of a castle often kept a pack of hounds but another form of hunting for small animals such as rabbits was with birds called falcons. These birds were very expensive and valuable. Books on how to keep, breed and hunt with birds of prey, as they are known, were popular reading for those who went hunting. Almost any animal that lived in the woods or in the open countryside could be hunted—deer, boar, bears, wolves, partridges, pheasants and foxes. Stags were hunted by using the hounds to chase them out of the woods where the huntsmen stood with bows and arrows or crossbows. Another way was to set up nets. The hounds would chase the stag into the net where it was trapped. Hunting could also be dangerous and sometimes animals such as boar would turn and bite the hunter. In the Middle Ages people used to try to hide when they went hunting, by sticking twigs and leaves in their hats and on their clothing. There are even stories of people who dressed up as deer so that they could creep up closer to the animals. At the end of a day's hunting, the hunt party would return to the castle with the animals they had caught.

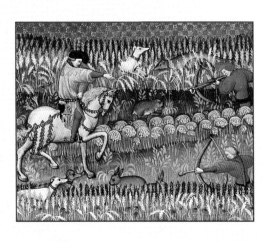

If Stones could talk...

Even if it may seem that castles were built to last forever, many families left their castles at the end of the Middle Ages and, over many years, these castles fell into ruin. In many cases the owners no longer had enough money to look after the castle and had to leave. Others left for just the opposite reason: they had so much money that they could build a more modern and comfortable home. Many noble families found it nicer to live in a grand town house than in an isolated and draughty castle. Because of their thick walls old castles were sometimes turned into prisons—and a lot of stories were written about dark dungeons and torture chambers. In most cases, however, the castles slowly became ruins. But even these ruins often tell us how proud the castle must have been in its time.

The Illustrations in this Book

Pages 2–3:

Marksburg Castle, Germany, photograph (background), photo by Detlef Oster, Lahnstein

Limbourg Brothers, calendar page **September** from the *Très Riches Heures* of Jean Duc de Berry, *c.* 1410–16, Musée Condé, Chantilly

Eltz Castle, Germany, photograph (background), photo by Pavel Vácha

Paolo Uccello, **St George and the Dragon**, *c.* 1439–40, tempera on panel, 52 x 90 cm, Musée Jacquemart-André, Paris

Pages 4–5:

Bodiam Castle, England, photograph, photo by NTPL/Unichrome

Chillon Castle, Switzerland, photograph, photo by Ondrej Kavan

Kaiserburg (Emperor's Castle), Nuremberg, Germany, photograph

Tarasp Castle, Switzerland, photograph

Caesar's Tower, Provins, France, photograph, photo by Pavel Vácha

Krak des Chevaliers, Syria, photograph, photo by Dr. Joachim Zeune

Page 9:

The Zürcher arm themselves against the Schwyzer by Erecting Fortifications (Extracting wood from the forest), from the *Official Chronicle of Bern* of Dietbold Schilling, fifteenth century, Burgerbibliothek Bern

Beginning the Construction of the Minster in Bern in 1420, from the *Official Chronicle of Bern* of Dietbold Schilling, fifteenth century, Burgerbibliothek Bern

Pages 10–11:

Building a Tower (representation of a jib crane and a treadmill), fol. 9v from the *World Chronicle* of Rudolf von Ems, 1383, Württembergische Landesbibliothek, Stuttgart

Page 13:

The Bathhouse, fols. 18v–19r from the collection of the Princes of Waldburg Wolfegg, *c.* 1480, Wolfegg near Ravensburg, Germany

Page 15:

Clockwise: Details from

Story of the beautiful Prokris, Wife of Kephalos, fol. 39v, from Boccaccio's *Des femmes nobles*, *c.* 1401, Bibliothèque nationale, Paris

Story of Pamphilla, Daughter of Plateus, fol. 69r from Boccaccio's *Des femmes nobles*, *c.* 1401, Bibliothèque nationale, Paris

Mr Goeli (Backgammon), fol. 262v from the *Codex Manesse*, mid-fourteenth century, Universitätsbibliothek Heidelberg

Hockey Game, Musée Condé de Chantilly

Thamar, the most noble Paintress, fol. 86r from Boccaccio's *Des femmes nobles*, *c.* 1401, Bibliothèque nationale, Paris

Delivery of the Gambling Debt, fol. 273 from Boccaccio's *Decamerone*, 9th day, 4th tale in the French translation of Laurent de Premierfait of 1414, Vaticana, Rome (also p. 14)

Mr Reinmar the Fiddler, fol. 312r from the *Codex Manesse*, mid-fourteenth century, Universitätsbibliothek Heidelberg

Margrave Otto von Brandenburg (Chess), fol. 13r from the *Codex Manesse*, mid-fourteenth century, Universitätsbibliothek Heidelberg

Story of Gala Cyrilla, Wife of King Tarquinius, fol. 71r from Boccaccio's *Des femmes nobles*, *c.* 1401, Bibliothèque nationale, Paris

Christine de Pizan, Picture of the author, from the *Book of the City of Women*, 1405

Game of Dice, fol. 273 from Boccaccio's *Decamerone*, 9th day, 4th tale in the French translation of Laurent de Premierfait of 1414, Vaticana, Rome (also p. 14)